IN MEMORY OF:

    Roger E. Allen

PRESENTED BY:

Mr. & Mrs. Joseph Talarico

About the Author

Widely published historian and literary scholar Don Nardo has written or edited numerous books about Shakespeare's plays and characters. He has also acted in several productions of the Bard's plays staged by the National Shakespeare Company and other troupes. Mr. Nardo lives with his wife, Christine, in Massachusetts.

Index

acting companies, 11–12, 14, 15–17
Allen, Gyles, 17, 20–21
audience, 35, 37, 39

Bankside (London, England), 19–20
Brend, Sir Nicholas, 19
building materials, 20–21
Burbage, Cuthbert, 14, 17, 19–21
Burbage, James, 14–17
Burbage, Richard, 14, 17, 19–21, 27

cannon fire, 40
costumes, 36

design, 22–23
destruction, 40, 42
discovery area, 30–31

Earl of Worcester's Men, 11

foundation, 23
frame, 23–24

groundlings, 39

Hamlet, 39–40
Heavens, 28–29, 30
Hell, 28
Heminge, John, 19
Henry V, 9, 36, 37
Henry VIII, 40
hut, 29–30

land, 19–20, 22
Leicester's Men, 14, 16
London theaters, 11, 12, 40, 42
  see also specific theaters
Lord Chamberlain's Men, 15–16

Mendilow, A.A., 11–12

new Globe Theater, 9

platform, 11–12, 27–29, 30–31
Puritans, 40, 42

Queen's Men, 11, 14

Romeo and Juliet, 32
roof, 25, 32
Rose, the, 20

sets, 36, 37

Shakespeare, William, 12, 14–16, 19, 42
Shakespeare Globe Playhouse Trust, 9
size, 39
Smith, Irwin, 30–31
soundings, 39
Southwark (London, England), 7, 20
special effects, 39–40
stage, 11–12, 27–29, 30–31
Streete, Peter, 21–22
surveyor's line, 22
Swan, the, 33

Theatre, the, 15, 17, 20–23
tiring house, 27–28, 30–33
trapdoors, 28, 29–30, 39–40

walls, 24, 32
Wanamaker, Sam, 7–9
weather, 35
women, 37

yard, 27, 39

For More Information

Books

Aliki, *William Shakespeare and the Globe*. New York: HarperCollins, 1999.

Colleen Angesen and Margie Blumeberg, *Shakespeare for Kids: His Life and Times: 21 Activities.* Chicago: Chicago Review, 1999.

Peter Chrisp, *Welcome to the Globe: The Story of Shakespeare's Theater.* London: Dorling Kindersley, 2000.

Julie Ferris, *Shakespeare's London: A Guide to Elizabethan London.* New York: Kingfisher, 2000.

Jacqueline Morley, *Shakespeare's Theater*. New York: Peter Bedrick, 1994.

J.R. Mulryne, *Shakespeare's Globe Rebuilt*. New York: Cambridge University Press, 1997.

Diane Yancey, *Life in the Elizabethan Theater*. San Diego: Lucent, 1997.

Web Sites

Architectural Information on the Current Reconstruction of the Globe Theater (www.sgc.umd.edu/arch.htm). Provides several links to sites describing various aspects of the 1990s reconstruction of the Globe Theater.

The Globe Theater: A Brief History (www.calvin.edu/academic/engl/346/proj/nathan/globe.htm). A good brief overview of the Globe, with links to related topics.

Mr. William Shakespeare and the Internet (http://shakespeare.palomar.edu). A tremendous resource that guides students to many of the best online sites containing information about Shakespeare, his times, his plays, and the Globe Theater.

Glossary

auger—A hand drill used to bore holes in wood.

capitals—The decorative tops of pillars.

discovery area—The rear stage, located in the lowest level of the tiring house.

first sounding—A trumpet blast signaling that a performance was about to begin.

groundlings—Spectators who stood in the yard in the Globe and other Elizabethan theaters.

Heavens—A wooden awning, or ceiling, located about 30 feet (9 meters) above the stage.

Hell—The area beneath the stage, from which characters such as ghosts made their entrances.

hut—Located directly above the Heavens, an enclosed area that housed equipment for lowering actors on ropes and creating special sound effects.

laths—Vertical branches woven into the wattle in the wattle-and-daub construction method.

platform—The front stage in an Elizabethan theater.

platts—Blueprints for construction projects.

polygon—A many-sided figure or structure.

sills—Large timber beams that rested horizontally on a building's foundation and bore the weight of the rest of the structure.

surveyor's line—A measuring rope that was one of the standard tools of builders in late medieval England.

tiring house—A rectangular structure located directly behind the stage, it housed the rear stage, dressing rooms for the actors, and the prop storage.

wattle-and-daub—A construction technique in which twigs or branches are interwoven and then covered by a pastelike plaster.

yard—The open area on three sides of the stage in the central part of an Elizabethan theater.

Chronology

1564 William Shakespeare is born in Stratford, England.

1576 Noted actor and theatrical manager James Burbage builds the Theatre, the first public theater erected in Europe since ancient times.

1594 James Burbage forms a new acting company, the Lord Chamberlain's Men; Shakespeare soon becomes a shareholder in the company.

1598 Burbage's sons, Richard and Cuthbert, gain the financing to build a new theater—the Globe.

1599 The Globe is built and opens to the public with a production of Shakespeare's *Henry V*.

1613 The Globe burns down after sparks from a cannon ignite the thatch roof; however, the theater is quickly rebuilt.

1616 William Shakespeare dies.

1642 The Globe closes permanently, along with other London theaters, because the Puritans, temporarily in power in the city, see most forms of entertainment as ungodly.

1644 The Globe is torn down to make way for apartment buildings.

1949 American actor Sam Wanamaker visits London for the first time and conceives the bold idea of reconstructing the Globe.

1993 After years of diligent planning and fund-raising by Wanamaker and others, construction begins on the new Globe.

1997 The newly rebuilt Globe Theater, based as much as possible on the original, is inaugurated in a gala ceremony presided over by Queen Elizabeth II.

Notes

Chapter 1: An Urgent Need for a New Theater
1. A.A. Mendilow, "The Elizabethan Theater," in A.A. Mendilow and Alice Shalvi, *The World and Art of Shakespeare*. New York: Daniel Davey, 1967, p. 26.

Chapter 2: The Land, Foundation, Walls, and Roof
2. Quoted in William Archer and W.J. Lawrence, "The Playhouse," in *Shakespeare's England: An Account of the Life and Manners of His Age*, vol. 2. Oxford, UK: Clarendon, 1966, p. 284.
3. Quoted in Irwin Smith, *Shakespeare's Globe Playhouse: A Modern Reconstruction*. New York: Scribner's, 1975, p. 34.

Chapter 3: The Stage: Under, Over, and Behind
4. Smith, *Shakespeare's Globe Playhouse*, p. 75.
5. Smith, *Shakespeare's Globe Playhouse*, p. 105.
6. Quoted in Smith, *Shakespeare's Globe Playhouse*, p. 52.

Chapter 4: Play Production in the Globe
7. William Shakespeare, *Henry V*, act 1, scene 1, lines 12–13, 19.
8. Quoted in Andrew Gurr, *Playgoing in Shakespeare's London*. New York: Cambridge University Press, 1987, p. 236.

An audience at the new Globe Theater waits for a play to begin. The inset shows actors performing Hamlet *in the same theater.*

much as they are partakers in the sins of the players and of the plays."[8] Two years later (in 1644), the Globe was demolished to make way for cheap apartment housing.

The glories of Shakespearean theater, born in the Globe and its sister theaters, did not die, however. After the Puritans fell from power, plays were once more presented in London. And in the years that followed, Shakespeare came to be recognized as one of the greatest playwrights who ever lived. Centuries later, his works inspired actor Sam Wanamaker so much that he decided to rebuild the Globe yet again. The Burbages, Shakespeare, and their fellow thespians did not know it at the time, but they had created a theatrical landmark for the ages.

digger hard at work in a hole he has dug. The actor playing the grave digger stood in Hell so that only his head and shoulders were visible to the audience.

Another common type of special effect was cannon fire. The use of the cannons located in the hut was not limited only to producing sound effects for battle scenes. In the finale of *Hamlet*, the cannons probably sounded as a salute as men solemnly carried Hamlet's dead body off the stage. The Elizabethans also had a custom of firing off guns and cannons during celebrations. In Shakespeare's *Henry VIII*, for example, cannons fired during an onstage banquet attended by the title character.

A Landmark for the Ages

Regrettably for Elizabethan actors and audiences, this cannon volley in *Henry VIII* led to the destruction of the original Globe Theater. During a performance of the play in 1613, sparks from one of the cannons ignited the thatched roof of the hut. The actors and spectators managed to escape unhurt. But the whole structure was destroyed.

Although the Globe was immediately rebuilt after the disaster, the new building's days were numbered. Only a few years later, in 1642, its doors closed permanently, along with those of London's other theaters. A civil war had recently brought the Puritans, an extremely conservative group, to power. And they strongly disapproved of actors and plays. One Puritan spokesman claimed that English playgoers brought themselves into "the danger of God's wrath . . . in as

Opposite:
This painting shows the famous grave digger scene from Shakespeare's Hamlet.

Most of the spectators entered the Globe through the front door. Many paid a penny, which was worth more than a modern penny but was still very reasonable and affordable. Because they stood in the dirt in the yard, they were known as groundlings. If someone wanted a seat in the galleries, he or she had to pay more. Modern estimates for the highest number of spectators the Globe could accommodate vary from fifteen hundred to twenty-five hundred.

When the theater was nearly full, a trumpet blast blared from the hut above the Heavens. Called the first sounding, it warned that the performance would soon begin. A couple of minutes later there was a second sounding and soon after that a third. Immediately after the third sounding, the play started.

A Taste of Special Effects

Usually the first scene of a play consisted mainly of actors engaging in conversation to set the scene. Sometimes, however, the spectators got a taste of special effects right away. In the opening scene of Shakespeare's *Hamlet*, for instance, the ghost of the title character's father appears on the battlements of a castle. As performed in the Globe, the trapdoor leading to Hell opened and the ghost stepped up onto the platform; meanwhile, stagehands up in the hut produced spooky sounds. Eventually, the ghostly figure exited the same way it had entered—through the trapdoor.

Later in the play, the trapdoor served a different purpose. In the scene in question, Hamlet and his friend Horatio visit a cemetery. They find a grave

Opposite: *Spectators watch a production of one of Shakespeare's plays.*

their own day, no matter what past era was being depicted. Another break with realism was the fact that women's parts were played by men (because society viewed it as improper for women to appear on stage).

In addition, the Globe's stage was most often bare, with no elaborate, painted sets. The members of the audience were expected to use their imaginations. Through some of the lines spoken by the actors, the playwright called on the audience to imagine that the action they were watching was actually taking place somewhere else. It might be a battlefield, a city street, or a mountainside.

One famous example of this verbal setting of the scene comes from the opening speech of Shakespeare's *Henry V*. "Can this cockpit [i.e., the theater] hold the vasty fields of France?" a narrator asks the spectators. The answer is obviously no. So he implores them: "On your imaginary forces work."[7] The Globe's stage and other structural elements were therefore intended as a sort of launching pad. During a performance, the playwright and actors did their best to transport the audience to another time and place.

Attracting an Audience

But before the actors could set the scene, they first had to draw the spectators into the theater. Flyers announcing an upcoming performance were plastered all over London. As an added measure, on the day of the show someone hoisted a white flag high above the theater's roof. Visible from most parts of the city, it signaled that a play was about to be staged.

"Your Thoughts Must Deck Our Kings"

In opening scenes of Elizabethan plays the actors often delivered lines that told the audience where the action of the play was supposed to take place. In his play *Henry V*, Shakespeare went a step further. He had a narrator open the play by asking the audience to use its imagination during the scenes that would follow. "On your imaginary forces work," the narrator says, and then adds:

> Suppose within the girdle of these walls are now confined two mighty monarchies [England and France in the 1400s, where the story is set].... Think when we talk of horses that you see them printing their proud hoofs in the receiving earth. For 'tis your thoughts that now must deck our kings [i.e., we leave it to your mind's eye to fill in the appropriate settings and atmosphere].

there were no lighting effects, and plays were almost always presented in the daytime.

"On Your Imaginary Forces Work"

Probably the biggest difference between theatricals then and now is the style of the settings. Today, most plays and movies go to great lengths to reproduce the costumes, buildings, and atmosphere of the time and place being portrayed. In a production about the Salem witch trials, for instance, the actors dress like the residents of Salem in the late 1600s. But in Shakespeare's Globe, the actors usually wore the clothes of

Chapter 4

Play Production in the Globe

ALL OF THE physical features built into the Globe—from the yard and platform below to the galleries, Heavens, and hut above—were designed with a specific purpose in mind. Each served one or more of the particular needs of play production in England during the Elizabethan Age. Theatrical events in that place and time were considerably different from today's Broadway plays, television shows, and movies.

For example, people today are used to enjoying such presentations while sitting in comfortable chairs in enclosed, climate-controlled homes and theaters. In contrast, many of the spectators in Elizabethan theaters had to stand for hours at a time. And the central sections of these structures were open to the elements. So if it rained hard, the performance had to be canceled. Also, there was no electricity. Consequently,

*Opposite:
A drawing from the 1600s shows actors performing on the Globe's platform while groundlings watch.*

of oak. It is also likely that the builders installed small pillars in the front wall of the tiring house. A surviving sketch of another London theater, the Swan, dating from circa 1596, shows such pillars lining the galleries. Though definitive proof is lacking, scholars think the Globe looked very much like the Swan.

These pillars, like the two big ones standing on the platform, were load-bearing and therefore functional. But they were also decorative. The carpenters added carved and painted capitals (top sections) to all the pillars. Other finishing touches of the Globe's construction included painting the Heavens (possibly done by Richard Burbage) and hanging festive curtains along the sides and tops of many of the galleries.

A Brand New Theater

There is no doubt that the first playgoers who attended the completed theater were impressed by this attention to detail and decoration. Several documents of that era mention the "beauty of the [tiring] houses and the stages," "our stately stage,"[6] or offer similar praises. The actors and playwrights must have been equally thrilled to have a brand new and elegant theater in which to work. At the time, they could not have foreseen that in the next few years the Globe would premiere some of the greatest plays ever written.

This illustration shows the Globe's sister theater, the Swan, as it looked in the early 1600s.

held musicians. But actors occasionally played scenes in them. Perhaps the best-known example was the balcony scene in *Romeo and Juliet*. The person playing Juliet stood in one of the rear galleries, while Romeo stood on the rear section of the platform.

Like the theater's outer walls, the walls of the tiring house were made of a wooden framework covered by wattle-and-daub. The walls were painted, possibly in bright colors. The tiring house's roof was thatched, like the roofs above the galleries and hut. And the doors in the lower level of the tiring house were made

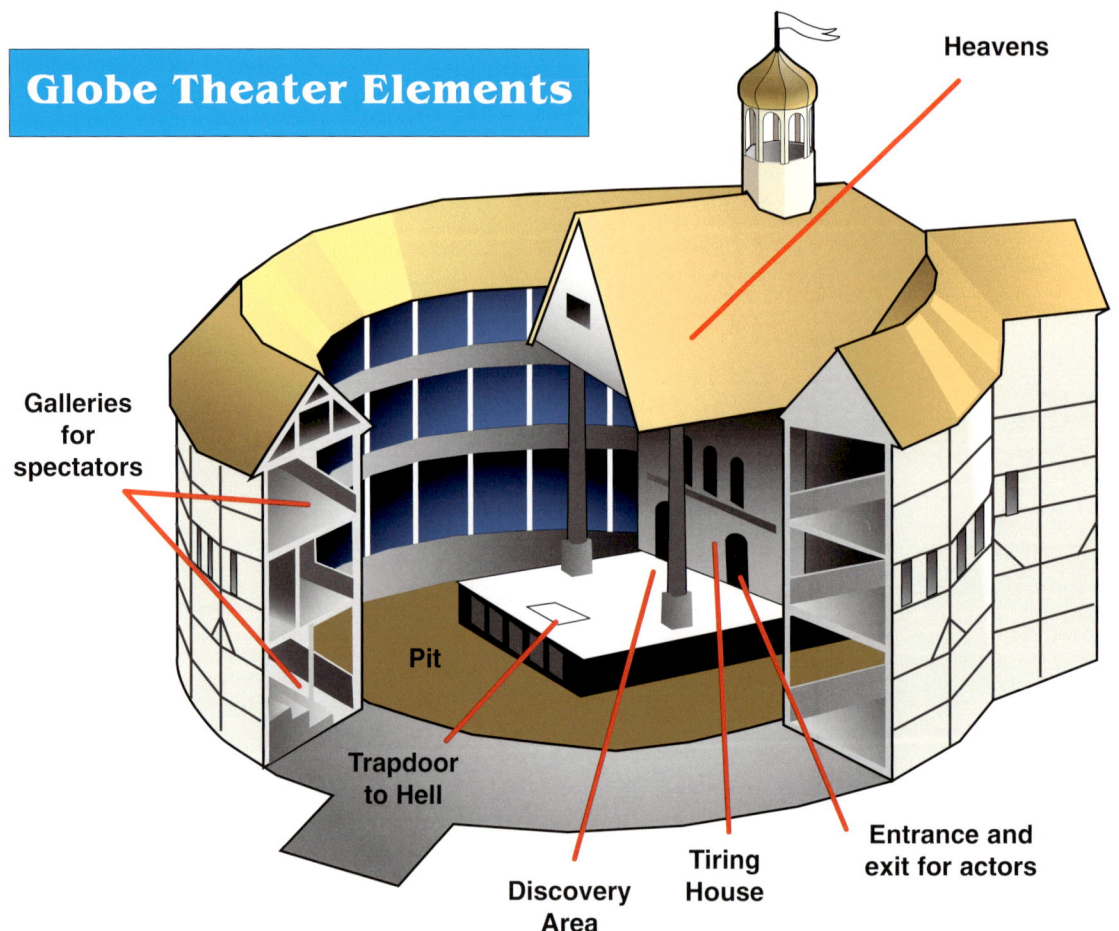

Globe Theater Elements

- Heavens
- Galleries for spectators
- Pit
- Trapdoor to Hell
- Discovery Area
- Tiring House
- Entrance and exit for actors

cause it was usually hidden by a curtain; and when someone drew back the curtain, a character or a new setting was discovered by, or revealed to, the audience. Generally, this setting was seen as separate and distant from the one on the platform. In the spectators' minds, the curtain represented an imaginary solid wall that separated the two settings. So, Smith explains, "it was never used as a means of entrance or exit."[5]

The two stories lying above the rear stage in the tiring house featured open galleries similar to those in which the spectators sat. Usually these rear galleries players to descend from the painted sky. The hut also held the cannon fired during battle scenes and the equipment that produced sound effects. About the latter, noted Shakespearean scholar Irwin Smith writes:

> The Elizabethan dramatist commonly called for thunder and lightning . . . trumpet blasts, falling chains, or other similar loud noises. Quite apart from the fact that such sounds helped to create an atmosphere of terror and torment, they served to drown out the noise made by the trap [door] mechanism.[4]

The Heavens and hut were held up in part by two huge pillarlike supports, each made from the trunk of a tree. These supports were plastered and painted bright colors to make them look decorative. The roof of the hut was steeply inclined and made of thatch.

The Tiring House

The second major section of the performing complex, the tiring house, was even more complex and time-consuming to build than the platform, Hell, and Heavens. The tiring house was rectangular and three stories high. Among its many features were at least two big, round-topped doors, one at the left rear, the other at the right rear of the platform. The actors made most of their regular entrances and exits through these doors.

Centered between the doors was a rear stage probably about 7 or 8 feet (about 2 or 2.5 meters) deep. It was sometimes called the discovery area. This was be-

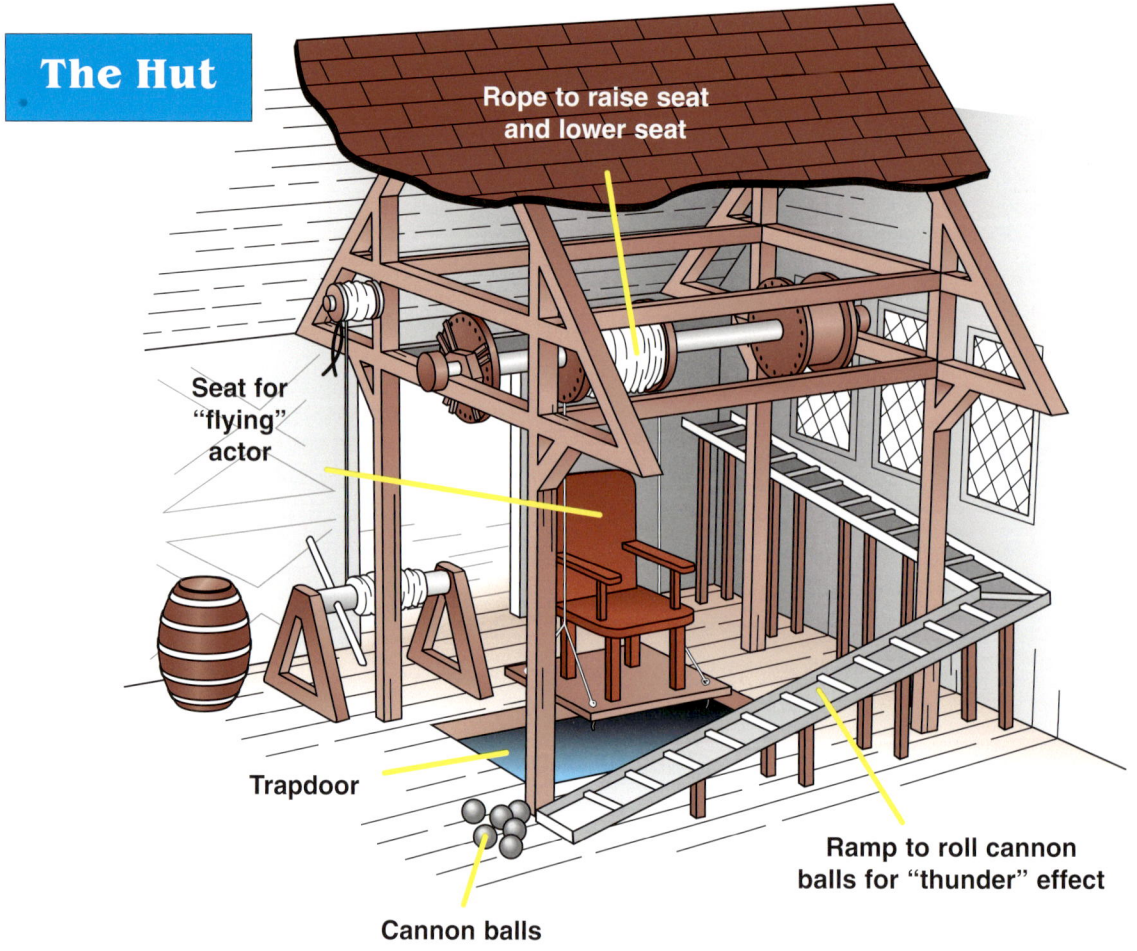

wooden awning, or ceiling, appropriately called the Heavens (or "shadow"). Soaring perhaps thirty feet (nine meters) above the actors, this ceiling featured painted stars, constellations, and clouds in imitation of the sky.

Directly above the Heavens was an enclosed, attic-like space generally referred to as the hut. The hut housed equipment, including ropes, which allowed the actors who played spirits and fairies seemingly to fly, another popular special effect. Streete constructed at least one trapdoor in the floor of the hut to allow these

29

the theater's outer perimeter. The tiring house held a second, rear stage, and it also housed dressing rooms for the actors and storage for props. Both the front stage and the tiring house had numerous structural and decorative features.

The Platform, Hell, and Heavens

Most scholars think that the front stage, the area so often called the platform, was constructed of pine boards. Estimates for its size vary. But it was most likely approximately 40 feet (12 meters) wide and 30 feet (9 meters) deep, giving the actors an ample playing area of some 1,200 square feet (111 square meters). The stage was raised about 5.5 to 6 feet (about 1.8 meters) off the ground level of the yard. And the outer edges of the platform featured a low railing, perhaps 18 inches (45 centimeters) high, that prevented the actors from falling off and injuring themselves. The railing also served as a deterrent to help keep spectators from climbing onto the stage.

In building the platform Streete and his men had to make allowances for the specific needs and common practices of play production. One of these practices was to have characters suddenly appear from beneath the platform, a kind of special visual effect. To accommodate their entrances, Streete installed an unknown number of trapdoors. Usually these characters were ghosts, devils, or other sinister sorts. So the area below the stage came to be called Hell.

Another challenge for the builders was a feature situated above rather than below the platform. It was a

Chapter 3

The Stage: Under, Over, and Behind

PETER STREETE AND his workmen devoted much of the eight-month construction period of the Globe to the stage, or platform. In this part of the process, some of the actors no doubt helped out. They could not only offer crucial advice about the proper shape and details of the playing area, but they also could put their artistic talents to good use. For instance, Richard Burbage was a gifted painter as well as a great actor.

Though referred to as the platform, the Globe's stage was much more than a mere group of wooden boards for the actors to stand on. It was part of what is best described as a performing complex that included two major sections. One was the front stage, which projected outward into the "yard," the central portion of the theater. The other major section was the tiring house, a separate structure that merged with

Opposite:
In this old engraving the Globe presents Shakespeare's A Midsummer Night's Dream.

 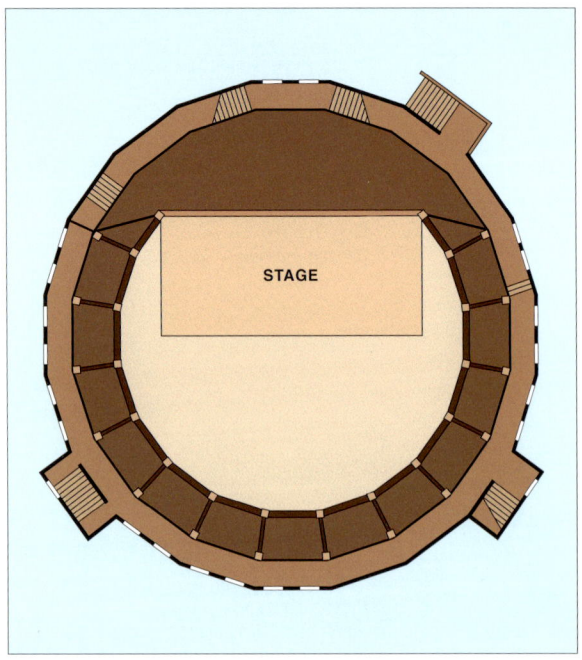

Meanwhile, as the daubers busied themselves on the building's perimeter, high above them their coworkers were laying the roof above the galleries. The roof supports were oak beams. Connecting the beams to the upper part of the frame were joints made by inserting wooden pegs in holes made by hand drills called augers. Atop the beams the workmen laid thatch, a mass of interwoven straw. The thatch was likely a foot (0.3 meters) or more in thickness and absorbed rainwater, keeping the people seated below it dry.

When the frame, galleries, walls, and roof were all in place, it was time to begin work on the heart of the theater. This was the stage on which the actors performed. As Peter Streete would learn in the months that followed, it was not only the most important part of the theater, but also structurally the most complex.

A floor plan (right) and exterior drawing (left) show the Globe as a many-sided structure.

dwell in houses built of sallow, willow, plum-tree, hardbeame, and elm. . . . But now all these are rejected, and nothing but oak any whit regarded."[3]

Constructing the Walls

While some workers were finishing the upper sections of the frame, others were starting to construct the first-story walls. The most common method then in use was wattle-and-daub. The wattle consisted of numerous tree branches, some of oak, others of hazel wood. The oak branches, called laths, were placed vertically about fifteen inches (thirty-eight centimeters) apart. Then the workmen interwove the hazel wood twigs horizontally through the laths, as in basket weaving. Finally came the daub, or plaster, which the workmen spread over the wattle lattice. The daub was a mixture of lime, sand, water, and chopped cow's hair.

This modern reconstruction of an old English house was built with wattle-and-daub materials.

More importantly, the specific shapes and measurements of the timbers taken from the Theatre demanded they be used in a nearly identical layout. The Theatre had been a three-story-high polygonal structure. In each story, galleries with seats for the spectators ran about two-thirds of the way around the circumference. These sections were roofed, but the central portion of the polygon was open to the sky. The circumstances dictated that the Globe would look the same.

The Foundation and Frame

The first task Streete and his crew likely undertook was to lay a sturdy foundation for the structure. This was necessary because the soil was soft, mainly because much of the area of Bankside had once been a marsh. Without a firm foundation, the structure would have sagged and slowly sunk into the ground over time. The foundation would have consisted of a series of piles—long, thick oak timbers similar to telephone poles. The workmen sunk the piles vertically into the ground as deep as they could.

With a firm foundation in place, the builders could begin erecting the frame. First they laid large oak timbers, called sills, horizontally on top of the foundation piles. The rest of the frame, which rose atop the sills, was built using a post-and-lintel technique. The posts were the vertical timber supports; the lintels were the horizontal ones. These were also made of oak, which, because of its hardness and durability, was then the mainstay of large-scale construction. A writer of that period stated, "In times past men were contented to

Measuring the Site

When Peter Streete and his construction crew arrived at Nicholas Brend's property in Bankside, their first task was to measure the land. They also used wooden stakes and ropes to make an outline in the dirt to indicate exactly where the theater would stand. To accomplish these steps, they used a tool called a surveyor's line. It was essentially a rope three "rods" long. In those days a rod, which measured 16 feet 6 inches (4.9 meters), was the standard unit of large-scale measure. (A one-rod-long measuring stick was called a perch.) Streete made sure that the measurements on the ground matched those called for in his platts (blueprints).

> The Globe's specific design and construction, as overseen by Streete, remains somewhat unclear. The original blueprints, in those days called platts, have not survived. And no detailed drawings of the structure have survived either. Modern reconstructions assume that Streete and his workmen employed the standard materials and techniques in use in England at that time.
>
> For the overall shape and layout of the new theater, Streete definitely chose a polygon (a many-sided figure). Some modern scholars think it had eight sides, making it octagonal; others suggest it had up to twenty sides, making it look almost circular. In any case, it must have fairly closely followed the plan of the Theatre. This was partly because the Theatre's layout, which was similar to that of other theaters in London, was seen as highly functional.

With this in mind, three days after Christmas in 1598 the Burbage brothers showed up at the Theatre accompanied by several carpenters and laborers. They proceeded to dismantle large sections of the structure. Allen got wind of what was happening and angrily insisted they stop. But legally there was nothing he could do. He did subsequently bring charges against the Burbages and claimed that they

> riotously assembled themselves together, and then and there armed themselves with diverse and many unlawful and offensive weapons . . . [and] attempted to pull down said Theatre . . . and having so done, did then also in the most forcible and riotous manner take and carry away from thence all the wood and timber . . . to Bankside.[2]

Circumstances Dictate the Layout

Allen's description of the dismantling of the Theatre was probably somewhat exaggerated. In fact, the workers likely tried to be as careful as possible to make sure the timbers and other materials were not damaged and could be reused in constructing the Globe. One thing Allen said was true, though. Burbage and the others carted what they had scavenged from the Theatre down to Brend's property at Bankside. There, they stacked everything off to one side while the builder the Burbages had hired prepared the site. He was a master carpenter named Peter Streete.

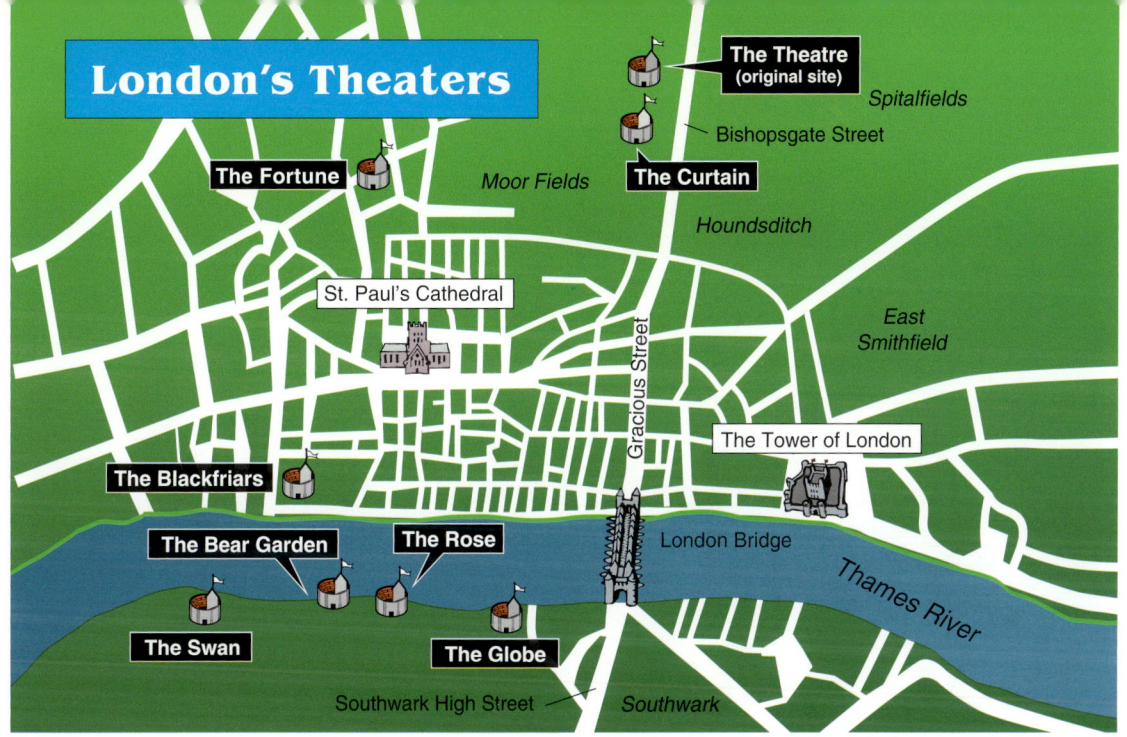

London Bridge. Bankside lay in Southwark, a region of London that still had plenty of open fields and trees. At the time, it was seen mainly as an entertainment center. There were a good many taverns, as well as archery ranges and theaters, including the Rose, which had been erected in 1587. In fact, Brend's property was located only a few hundred feet from the Rose.

After striking a deal with Brend late in 1598, the Burbages and their cohorts wasted no time in initiating the new project. They knew that some of the construction materials would have to be bought. But they also realized that they could save a considerable amount of money by cannibalizing parts of the existing Theatre. After all, technically Gyles Allen owned only the land on which that structure stood. He did not own the building itself, which had been financed by James Burbage's investors.

Chapter 2

The Land, Foundation, Walls, and Roof

Having pooled their money to finance the new theater, the Burbage brothers and their players looked forward to building it. But first, they had to find a suitable plot of land. They also had to locate the construction materials they would need at the cheapest prices possible. Finally, they had to decide on a design for both the stage area and the auditorium where the spectators would sit and stand. Once these preliminary steps were taken, the actual assembly of the structure took only eight months.

Land and Materials

As for the land, William Shakespeare and his fellow actor John Heminge knew a well-to-do individual, Sir Nicholas Brend, who had recently inherited a piece of property. It lay in a neighborhood called Bankside, located on the south shore of the Thames River near

Opposite: *This old sketch shows what London's Southwark looked like in Shakespeare's time.*

long after the formation of the Lord Chamberlain's Men company. Back in 1576 James Burbage had taken out a twenty-one-year lease on the property on which the Theatre stood. In the years that followed, he paid the owner of the land, Gyles Allen, a yearly rental fee. As the lease neared its end in the 1590s, the landlord began to give Burbage and his troupe a hard time. In drawing up the new lease, Allen made some outrageous demands, including a whopping 70-percent increase in the rental fee. He also stated that the building could be used as a theater for only five more years.

It was clear to the Burbages that signing a new lease with Allen would spell financial ruin for the company. To save the business, they had to find a way to build a new theater somewhere else. James Burbage died in 1597, before this dream could be realized. But his sons kept the dream alive in a novel way.

In 1598 Richard and Cuthbert Burbage approached the members of their troupe and offered them an unusual deal. If they would contribute some of the money needed for the new theater, they would receive in exchange a share in all future profits. Five members of the company, including William Shakespeare, agreed to provide funds. With this financial agreement, the groundwork was laid for the creation of what was to become one of the world's most famous theaters.

The man shown in this portrait is thought to be Richard Burbage.

of the Leicester's Men company. Shakespeare not only became a member of the new troupe, but he also purchased a share of it from the Burbages. By paying this money, he acquired the right to share in all company profits, giving him a modest but regular income.

Troubles with the Landlord

These moves by Shakespeare and the Burbages set a precedent. Before this, no actors in history had ever owned their own troupes. The next step was for the actors to dispense with outside investors, like those who had financed the Theatre, and own their own theaters.

The immediate events leading to construction of the first actor-owned theater—the Globe—began not

This early production of Shakespeare's As You Like It *was performed in the courtyard of an inn.*

money. But in fairly short order he managed to raise the necessary funds from outside investors, and in 1576 he erected the first public theater Europe had seen since ancient times. It was located about a mile (1.6 kilometers) north of the center of London and was called simply "the Theatre."

A second important milestone for the young William Shakespeare was financial in nature. In 1594 James Burbage formed a new acting company, the Lord Chamberlain's Men, taking with him most members

Actors perform on a portable stage before Queen Elizabeth I in her court.

prompter (a person who follows the script backstage and whispers the appropriate words to actors who have forgotten their lines). Another theory, which more scholars accept, contends that Shakespeare joined the Queen's Men after a big street fight. Supposedly one of the company's actors was injured in the brawl. And Shakespeare, more than willing to learn on the job, offered to take his place.

Two Important Career Milestones

However Shakespeare joined London's theatrical establishment, one thing is certain: He was a very quick learner. He was also a competent actor and a gifted playwright. By 1593, when he was only twenty-nine, he had gained a major reputation for writing *The Comedy of Errors, Richard III*, and other plays.

Two important milestones in Shakespeare's career occurred during these early years, both of which had a bearing on his later involvement in erecting the Globe. First, he met and became friendly with the Burbages, a prominent theatrical family. They included the father, James, and two sons—Richard and Cuthbert.

James Burbage had made history in 1574, when he had obtained permission from Queen Elizabeth I to present plays in London. At the time, he was the manager of the Leicester's Men acting company. Burbage recognized that a permanent theater building in the city was long overdue. And being a carpenter by trade, he had some specific ideas about how to create such a structure. What he lacked was

four sides as a rule, and perhaps had a canopy against the rain. . . . The whole cart was on wheels and constituted a traveling theater which could be set up in market squares and open spaces."[1] The actors and performances were sponsored by well-to-do earls and barons and, in time, also by small fees paid by the spectators.

As a child Shakespeare likely witnessed plays put on by such traveling companies. And many modern scholars think that these entertainments inspired him to pursue a theatrical career when he was older. In a way, then, a generation of actors who had no permanent theaters motivated a new generation that found a way to build them.

An Aspiring Young Playwright

The exact manner in which Shakespeare entered the theater remains unclear. He was born in 1564 in Stratford (now called Stratford-on-Avon), a village in central England. In his day, England was fast becoming one of the world's strongest and most influential nations. Several English cities had recently become successful commercial centers. And the largest, London, increasingly offered economic and cultural opportunities that attracted aspiring artists, poets, and dramatists.

By the time Shakespeare was in his teens, that city had also become the theatrical hub of the nation. He realized that the fastest way to achieve success as an actor and playwright was to move to London. And this he did sometime in the 1580s, probably when he was in his early twenties.

One theory holds that the young man's first job in the city was looking after horses outside a theater. Eventually the manager offered him a job as assistant

Opposite:
An engraving made long after Shakespeare's death shows the playwright at his writing desk.

Chapter 1

An Urgent Need for a New Theater

THE GLOBE THEATER and the company of actors who built it (including William Shakespeare) were part of a rich theatrical institution that thrived in London in the late 1500s and early 1600s. That institution had its roots in what was then fairly recent history. When Shakespeare and fellow performers were born in the mid–sixteenth century, England had no theaters. In fact, none existed anywhere in Europe.

The lack of formal theaters did not mean that no actors and plays existed, however. For mutual support, actors sometimes banded together into companies. The Queen's Men and the Earl of Worcester's Men were two prominent early examples. These companies traveled from place to place and presented plays on makeshift wooden stages they moved on horse-pulled carts. According to noted Shakespearean scholar A.A. Mendilow, such movable platforms were "open on all

Opposite:
In the early 1500s, a company of actors presents a play on a makeshift stage in a town square.

as possible. The problem was that none of the original designs had survived. And no one could say for sure what it had actually looked like or how it had been built.

Despite these and other daunting challenges, Wanamaker persevered. As the years went on, he told practically everyone he met on both sides of the Atlantic about his dream project. An important turning point occurred in 1970, when he established the Shakespeare Globe Playhouse Trust, designed to raise the necessary money. Slowly but steadily the funds accumulated. And in 1993 construction of the new Globe Theater began. Wanamaker died that same year. But the project went ahead and was completed in 1996. In May of the following year Queen Elizabeth II officially opened the theater, and it presented its first production—a rousing version of Shakespeare's *Henry V*.

The new Globe may not be a totally accurate replica of the original. And it may not sit on the exact location of the one Shakespeare and his companions erected. But it has significantly renewed modern popular interest in Shakespeare and Elizabethan play production. To Sam Wanamaker, it seemed a shame that a structure that had contributed so much to Western culture had disappeared forever. And his dedicated efforts in a sense resurrected it from oblivion. For London and its long and prestigious theatrical tradition, the wheel had truly come full circle.

been rebuilt. And he, like many other Americans, had always assumed that the English had thereafter taken pains to maintain it as a historic site. In fact, as Wanamaker discovered to his dismay, the Globe Theater had been gone for more than three centuries. Moreover, no one even knew exactly where it had stood.

In the weeks and months that followed, a grand and bold idea began to materialize in Wanamaker's mind. Somehow, no matter how long it took, he told himself, he would rebuild Shakespeare's theater. It was an incredibly ambitious, seemingly impossible plan for a young man with no money. Another formidable obstacle was that he wanted to reconstruct the Globe accurately—as close to the original design

An aerial photo taken in 2001 shows London's new Globe Theater.

Introduction

Resurrecting a Historic Structure

In 1949, American actor-director Sam Wanamaker made his first visit to London. The young man had long been an ardent fan of William Shakespeare's plays and had read many descriptions of their original productions in the late 1500s and early 1600s. These had taken place at the famous Globe Theater in Southwark, the section of Elizabethan London that contained the city's theater district. Not surprisingly, one of the first things Wanamaker wanted to do when he arrived in London was to pay a visit to the Globe.

The actor was sorely disappointed, however, when his cab driver informed him that the Globe no longer existed. How could this be, Wanamaker wondered. He knew that the original theater had burned down sometime in the 1600s. But it had quickly

Opposite: *American actor Sam Wanamaker tinkers with a model of the new Globe Theater.*

© 2005 Thomson Gale, a part of The Thomson Corporation.

Thomson and Star Logo are trademarks and Gale and Blackbirch Press are registered trademarks used herein under license.

For more information, contact
Blackbirch Press
27500 Drake Rd.
Farmington Hills, MI 48331-3535
Or you can visit our Internet site at http://www.gale.com

ALL RIGHTS RESERVED.
No part of this work covered by the copyright hereon may be reproduced or used in any form or by any means—graphic, electronic, or mechanical, including photocopying, recording, taping, Web distribution, or information storage retrieval systems—without the written permission of the publisher.

Every effort has been made to trace the owners of copyrighted material.

Photo credits:
Cover image: © North Wind Pictures
AP/Wide World Photos, 42 (main)
© W. Cody/CORBIS, 24
© Christopher Cormack/CORBIS, 6
Dulwich Picture Gallery, London/Bridgeman Art Library, 17
© Jason Hawkes/CORBIS, 8
© Hulton/Archive by Getty Images, 16
© Robbie Jack/CORBIS, 42 (inset)
Mary Evans Picture Library, 18
© North Wind Pictures, 10, 13, 15, 25 (left), 26, 32, 34
© Stock Montage, Inc., 38, 41
Steve Zmina, 25 (right)

LIBRARY OF CONGRESS CATALOGING-IN-PUBLICATION DATA

Nardo, Don, 1947–
  The Globe Theater / by Don Nardo.
    p. cm. — (Building world landmarks)
  Includes bibliographical references and index.
  ISBN 1-4103-0560-0 (hard cover : alk. paper)
  1. Globe Theatre (London, England : 1599–1644) 2. Shakespeare, William, 1564–1616—Stage history—To 1625. 3. Shakespeare, William, 1564–1616—Stage history—England—London. 4. Theaters—England—London—History—17th century. 5. Theater—England—London—History—17th century. I. Title. II. Series.

PR2920.N37 2005
792'.09421'64   2004027706

Printed in the United States of America
10 9 8 7 6 5 4 3 2 1

BUILDING WORLD LANDMARKS

The Globe Theater

by Don Nardo

BLACKBIRCH PRESS
An imprint of Thomson Gale, a part of The Thomson Corporation

Table of Contents

Introduction
Resurrecting a Historic Structure 7

Chapter 1
An Urgent Need for a New Theater 11

Chapter 2
The Land, Foundation, Walls, and Roof 19

Chapter 3
The Stage: Under, Over, and Behind 27

Chapter 4
Play Production in the Globe 35

Notes 43

Chronology 44

Glossary 45

For More Information 46

Index 47

About the Author 48

Other titles in the Building World Landmarks series include:

The Akashi-Kaikyo Bridge
The Arc d' Triomphe
The Aswan High Dam
The Berlin Wall
The Guggenheim Museum Bilbao
The London Tower Bridge
The Panama Canal
The Petronas Towers
The Royal Gorge
The Sydney Opera House

The Globe Theater